Big Six

MATHEWSON, N.Y., NAT'L

TINKER, CHI., NAT'L

NORWORTH, N.Y., AUTH.

VON TILZER, N.Y., COMP.

TAKE ME OUT TO THE BALL GAME
BY JACK NORWORTH

KATIE CASEY WAS BASE-BALL MAD
HAD THE FEVER AND HAD IT BAD,
JUST TO ROOT FOR THE HOME ~~TEAM~~ TOWN CREW
EVERY SUE — KATIE BLEW
ON A SATURDAY, HER ~~FRIEND JOE~~ YOUNG BEAU
CALLED TO SEE IF SHE'D LIKE TO GO
TO SEE A SHOW, BUT MISS ~~KATE~~ SAID NO,
I'LL TELL YOU WHAT YOU CAN DO —

TAKE ME OUT TO THE BALL GAME
TAKE ME OUT ~~TO~~ WITH THE ~~PARK~~ CROWD
BUY ME SOME PEANUTS AND CRACKERJACK
I DON'T CARE IF I NEVER GET BACK
LET ME ROOT, ROOT, ROOT FOR THE HOME TEAM,
IF THEY DON'T WIN ITS A SHAME,
FOR ITS ONE, TWO, THREE STRIKES, YOUR OUT
AT THE OLD BALL GAME

Jack Norworth's original manuscript for "Take Me Out to the Ball Game" (courtesy of National Baseball Hall of Fame Library, Cooperstown, N.Y.)

THE SENSATIONAL BASEBALL SONG

TAKE ME OUT
TO THE
BALL GAME

LYRICS BY
JACK NORWORTH

MUSIC BY
ALBERT VON TILZER

JIM BURKE

Introduction by Pete Hamill

LITTLE, BROWN AND COMPANY
New York ∞ Boston

This book is dedicated to my father, Thomas Burke, and Bill Marvin,
my first baseball coaches in North Little League,
Manchester, New Hampshire.
Go Sluggers!
—J. B.

Special thanks to Mary Gruetzke, who creatively suggested Norworth's lyrics; Andrea Spooner for her insightful editing; and Alyssa Morris for her sharp design.
To Pete Hamill, the very gifted quintessential New Yorker, with whom I'm thrilled to work. To my wonderful models: from the Wojtukiewicz Family: Samantha,
James, and Taylor. To Alec and Evan Chyriwski; Paul Del Rossi, Graham Howarth, Rand Webb, Richard Broderick, Angelo Anobile, Doug Chayka, Josh George,
Michael Arenella, and John M. Serafinko. Thanks also to Pattie Wojtukiewicz and Tara O'Boyle. A "stadium's cheer" to the folks at The National Baseball
Hall of Fame Library in Cooperstown, New York: Claudette Burke for her fact checking and Bill Burdick for locating references in their collection.
Also thanks to Bob Bluthardt from The Ballparks Committee, the Society for American Baseball Research, archivist Carey Stumm from
the New York Transit Museum, and a tip of the hat to Helen Uffner Vintage Clothing, in New York City.

Paintings copyright © 2006 by Jim Burke
Introduction copyright © 2006 by Pete Hamill
Song lyrics by Jack Norworth
All other text copyright © 2006 by Jim Burke

Cracker Jack® is a registered trademark of Frito-Lay, Inc.

Little, Brown and Company

Time Warner Book Group
1271 Avenue of the Americas, New York, NY 10020
Visit our Web site at www.lb-kids.com

First Edition: March 2006

Library of Congress Cataloging-in-Publication Data

Burke, Jim.
   Take me out to the ball game / by Jim Burke ; lyrics by Jack Norworth ; introduction by
Pete Hamill.—1st ed.
   p. cm.
   ISBN 0-316-75819-1
   1. Baseball—United States—Miscellanea—Juvenile literature. 2. Baseball—United States—
History—Juvenile literature. 3. Von Tilzer, Albert. Take me out to the ball game. I. Burke,
Jim, ill. II. Von Tilzer, Albert. Take me out to the ball game. Text. III. Title.
GV873.N67 2006
796.357—dc22   2005003826

10 9 8 7 6 5 4 3 2 1

PHX

Printed in China

The paintings for this book were done in oil on gessoed masonite board.
The endpaper illustrations were done in pencil and acrylic washes on bristol board.
The text was set in Carlton and Golden Cockerel, and the display type is New Modern Classic.

THE SONG OF SUMMER

An Introduction by Pete Hamill

Once upon a time, there was another America, and its game was baseball.

In those distant years before World War I, there was no radio, no television, no movie newsreels with sound tracks. Across the months of good weather, boys (and a few girls) played the game in sandlots and open fields. Most could only imagine seeing it played by the storied professionals—Walter Johnson or Honus Wagner or the great Christy Mathewson. If they lived far from cities, they might never see such a game or any of its heroes. They read about the professionals in the newspapers, but they could only dream of going to the big league ballparks.

In 1908, the year in which *Take Me Out to the Ball Game* was written, the greatest of all ballparks in New York was called the Polo Grounds. For thousands of young people, that ballpark became a place of American possibility, the true field of dreams, for in that year, the great flood of European immigrants was at high tide. The new arrivals, most of them young and full of hope, were jamming Manhattan, living in rat-infested tenements, trying to become Americans. Baseball would help teach them. The subway had just begun service four years prior, and the ballpark was just a train ride away: one of the only places in their urban world that offered simple beauty. Here were green grass, rules and order, and a field that seemed to shut out the imperfect city that surrounded it.

But baseball in 1908 was very much like the country where it flourished; the time was simpler, yet far from perfect. Women still could not vote. Many newcomers and African Americans had to endure persecution at the hands of those who insisted that these groups were "not like us." Almost forty years would pass before Jackie Robinson became the first black player to walk out on the sweet green grass of a Major League ballpark. Robinson didn't just integrate baseball; he integrated the stands. And when that happened, the United States of America changed forever. Regardless of heritage, we could all sing "Take Me Out to the Ball Game" and mean it. We could all root, root, root for the home team. Together. And we still do today.

These days, the site of the Polo Grounds is a housing project in upper Manhattan, and almost nobody alive ever saw Christy Mathewson pitch. But there are millions of us who got to see Willie Mays, the last great hero of the New York Giants, when he came to the Polo Grounds in those first glad years of the 1950s. I can see Mays now, running and running and running, deep into center field, in glorious pursuit of a fly ball that will not escape him. I am eating peanuts and Cracker Jack. I don't care if I never get back.

And all of the greats will keep playing forever in the American memory. This book pays tribute to one of these legends—Christy Mathewson—who helped shape the game of baseball, and whose character, class, and athletic feats should be remembered always.

—P. H.

Photo: The Polo Grounds, 1905 (courtesy of National Baseball Hall of Fame Library, Cooperstown, N.Y.)

NEW YORK CITY, 1908

In a season of record-breaking attendance at ball games across the country, the New York Giants drew the largest crowds by far, easily surpassing three quarters of a million spectators that year. New Yorkers cheered for their Giants with a feverish pitch, and store owners even closed shops to root for the home team.

While riding Manhattan's Ninth Avenue elevated subway line overlooking the cherished Giants' baseball field, entertainer Jack Norworth found inspiration in a poster that read BASE BALL TODAY—POLO GROUNDS. Though he had never been to a game, he captured the jubilant stadium-bound fans' excitement in lyrics that he quickly jotted on a scrap of paper. Composer Albert Von Tilzer later created the melody for the soon-to-be hit song, which has forever since been linked to America's favorite pastime. AND IT GOES LIKE THIS . . .

Katie Casey was base ball mad.
Had the fever and had it bad;
Just to root for the home town crew,
Ev'ry sou Katie blew.

Fascination for one particular player
during this era remains: Christy Mathewson,
the greatest pitcher in New York Giants history.
Known to fans as "Matty," he was feared by opponents and respected by umpires — but he was
also referred to as "The Christian Gentleman" for
promising his mother not to play ball on Sundays.
With a reputation for clean living and good
sportsmanship, this newspaper headliner was
America's first sports superstar and the ideal role
model for the nation's youth. Mathewson was a
college-educated athlete who was also a standout
on the football team at Bucknell University,
where he maintained an A average. He was also a
passionate checkers player who once beat world
champion Newell Banks.

*A note about the lyrics: In 1908, "baseball" was written as two
words; the word "sou" refers to a small amount of money.*

On a Saturday, her young beau
Called to see if she'd like to go,
To see a show, but Miss Kate said,
"No, I'll tell you what you can do.

In the 1870s, polo was played in an area just north of Central Park. Taken over by baseball in 1883, the park was shared by the New Yorks (later called the Giants) of the National League and the Metropolitans of the American Association. The name "Polo Grounds" remained through two moves, and by 1908, the bathtub-shaped ballpark was located between 157th and 159th Streets near the Harlem River. A rock ledge overlooking the park, known as Coogan's Bluff, provided free partial views of the field to thousands on game day.

Adding to the folklore of the Polo Grounds, it's believed that the term "hot dog" may have been coined there in 1901 by cartoonist Tad Dorgan, who drew a picture of what was then called a Dachshund sausage. Forgetting how to spell it, he labeled it a "hot dog" instead.

A note about the lyrics: The word "beau" means a woman's or girl's boyfriend.

Take me out to the ball game,
Take me out with the crowd.
Buy me some peanuts
and Cracker Jack,
I don't care if I never get back,

On September 23, 1908, some twenty thousand eager fans spun the turnstiles to witness what may forever remain one of sports' most remarkable matchups and most controversial contests in baseball history. The New York Giants, managed by the fiery John McGraw, hosted the reigning World Series champs, archrival Chicago Cubs, during the National League pennant race to determine who would play in the 1908 World Series. Not only did they share an explosive rivalry, but also powerful pitching rosters. The contest dueled fireballer Christy Mathewson against stellar southpaw Jack "The Giant Killer" Pfiester, a nickname earned through his victories against the New York club.

"Our greatest chance ... lies in the fact that we will finish the season at home. The encouragement of a friendly big city is no small factor in a team's success."
—Christy Mathewson

Let me

ROOT,

ROOT,

ROOT

for the home team,

If they don't win it's a shame.

"Mathewson was the greatest pitcher who ever lived. He had the knowledge, judgment, perfect control, and form. It was wonderful to watch him pitch— when he wasn't pitching against you."

—Connie Mack, Baseball Hall of Fame inductee, 1937

Long before radio, television, or the Internet, daily newspapers covered games and their players with painstaking detail and a contagious enthusiasm, often creating colorful nicknames for characters of the field. The frequent subject of sports journalism, Christy Mathewson was nicknamed "Big Six" after New York City's then most reliable fire station, Americus Engine Company No. 6. (Another theory of the name's origin was the player's height of 6 feet 1-1/2 inches, exceptional in an era when the average ballplayer stood at just 5 feet 7 inches tall.) When "Big Six" stood on the mound, fans felt that their team deserved to win.

For it's **ONE, TWO, THREE** strikes, you're out,
At the old ball game."

change of pace

fastball

fadeaway

"I always try to give that batter exactly the pitch he least expects to get," Mathewson once noted. His pitches included the fastball, the change of pace, and the fadeaway.

The fastball is thrown at full speed with a whiplike action from a flick of the wrist, coming off the fingertips and rocketing directly to the catcher. The change of pace is delivered much like a fastball, but without the whiplike action in the wrist. The position of the fingers and thumb also causes the ball to slow down. Expecting a fastball, the batter starts to swing, only to identify the slow ball when it's too late. The fadeaway is referred to today as the screwball. The pitch is delivered with an unnatural counterclockwise snap of the wrist that causes the ball to drop down and curve inward on a right-handed batter (or down and outward on a left-handed batter). Matty claimed that it was the ball that had won for him all of his baseball honors.

Katie Casey saw all the games,
Knew the players by their first names,

In those days players neither wore numbers nor names on the back of their uniforms, but, idolized by fans, they were instantly recognized. And fans like Katie Casey would memorize all of the players' statistics just as thoroughly as people do today.

1908 New York Giants Team Roster

REGULARS

1B   Fred Tenney

2B   "Laughing" Larry Doyle

SS   Al Bridwell

3B   Art Devlin

OF   "Turkey" Mike Donlin

OF   Cy Seymour

OF   Spike Shannon

C   Roger "The Duke of Tralee" Bresnahan

PITCHERS

R   Christy "Big Six" Mathewson

L   Hooks Wiltse

R   Doc Crandall

R   Joe "Iron Man" McGinnity

R   Luther Taylor

R   Leon "Red" Ames

Managed by John "the Little Napoleon" McGraw

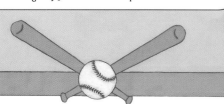

Told the umpire he was wrong,
All along good and strong.

When the score was just two to two,
Katie Casey knew what to do,

Because "Matty" was one of the most
respected players in the game, umpires often
awaited his nod of approval to gauge the accuracy
of their calls.

The first umpire to raise his right hand, signaling
a strike, is believed by many to have been Cy
Rigler in 1905. By 1908, the umpire hand signals
were becoming standard, making the games easier
to follow for fans.

The first hand signals between team members
were introduced by this Giants team under
manager John McGraw. In order to communicate
with a deaf teammate, pitcher Luther Taylor,
McGraw insisted that players learn the sign
language alphabet.

A note about the lyrics: In the song, "the score was just two to two," but during the game featured in this book, the score was actually one to one going into the bottom of the ninth inning.

Just to cheer up the boys she knew,
She made the gang sing this song:

"Take me out to the ball game,
Take me out to the crowd.
Buy me some peanuts and Cracker Jack,
I don't care if I never get back.

"Chicago boasts a crackerjack pitching staff, and has a hard hitting, fast fielding, heady, aggressive team. I believe the Giants outgame the Cubs, and I think this will win the pennant for us."

—Christy Mathewson

A unique combination of popcorn, peanuts, and molasses was introduced in 1893 at Chicago's first World's Fair by the F.W. Rueckheim and Brother Company. In 1896, Rueckheim's brother and partner, Louis, discovered a process for keeping the morsels from sticking together. After sampling the new treat, a salesman exclaimed, "That's crackerjack!" The name was soon trademarked, and later immortalized in Norworth's lyrics.

Another Chicago "first" was the electronic scoreboard, invented by George Baird in the same year as this 1908 contest.

Let me
ROOT,
ROOT,
ROOT
for the home team,
If they don't win it's a shame.

Within this fierce Giants-Cubs rivalry developed a thunderous, much-publicized battle between Matty and Chicago's ace shortstop, Joe Tinker. In their early duels, Tinker was an easy out for Matty. His short, quick swings were useless against Matty's low curveball, until Tinker finally figured out that by stepping back from the plate and sliding his hands toward the handle end of a longer bat, he'd allow his swing enough change of pace to smash the curveball and crack Big Six's fastball. "I've got your number now, Matty!" shouted Tinker once, thus becoming one of the very few batters who figured out how to consistently hit off Mathewson.

"Tinker became one of the most dangerous batters I have ever faced," Matty once wrote. In the 1908 season, Tinker hit 8 for 19 against the gifted ace.

In 1903, Big Six won thirty games and led the National League in strikeouts, an accomplishment he repeated again in 1904 and 1905. In the 1905 World Series, with catcher Roger Bresnahan, Matty delivered one of baseball's best post-season performances, shutting out the Philadelphia Athletics in Games 1, 3 and 5, allowing only fourteen total hits—a feat that still stands today as the greatest individual performance in World Series history. But the right-handed ace remained modest. "Anybody's best pitch is the one the batters ain't hitting that day," he once commented.

"Mathewson continued to hurl the ball into Bresnahan's mitt . . . [and] never lost control of the situation. He seemed to just breeze along under wraps."

—*New York Press*

TWO,

In 1908, the year Norworth wrote his most celebrated lyrics, Matty dazzled the nation by pitching his best season in professional ball: He had 37 wins, struck out 259 batters, had an earned run average of 1.43, and held opponents scoreless in 12 games. Destined for greatness, Mathewson was among the elite group of five first inducted into the Baseball Hall of Fame, along with Ty Cobb, Babe Ruth, Honus Wagner, and Walter Johnson.

"To a large extent it was Matty, more than anyone, who changed the public image of baseball and elevated it into the mainstream of American life."

— Lawrence Ritter

THREE
STRIKES,
you're out

"When a catcher in the Big League signals for a curved ball . . . he gets to know just how much the ball is going to curve. That is why the one catcher receives for the same pitcher so regularly, because they work together harmoniously."

—Christy Mathewson

In 1905, Matty's catcher, Roger "The Duke of Tralee" Bresnahan, was the first to try a batting helmet (then called a "pneumatic head protector") after being beaned. He's also credited with introducing shin guards for catchers into Major League Baseball in 1907, an idea sparked from the game of cricket. The Duke of Tralee, who was also an outstanding batter, was the first catcher to be inducted in the Baseball Hall of Fame, in 1945.

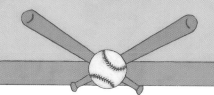

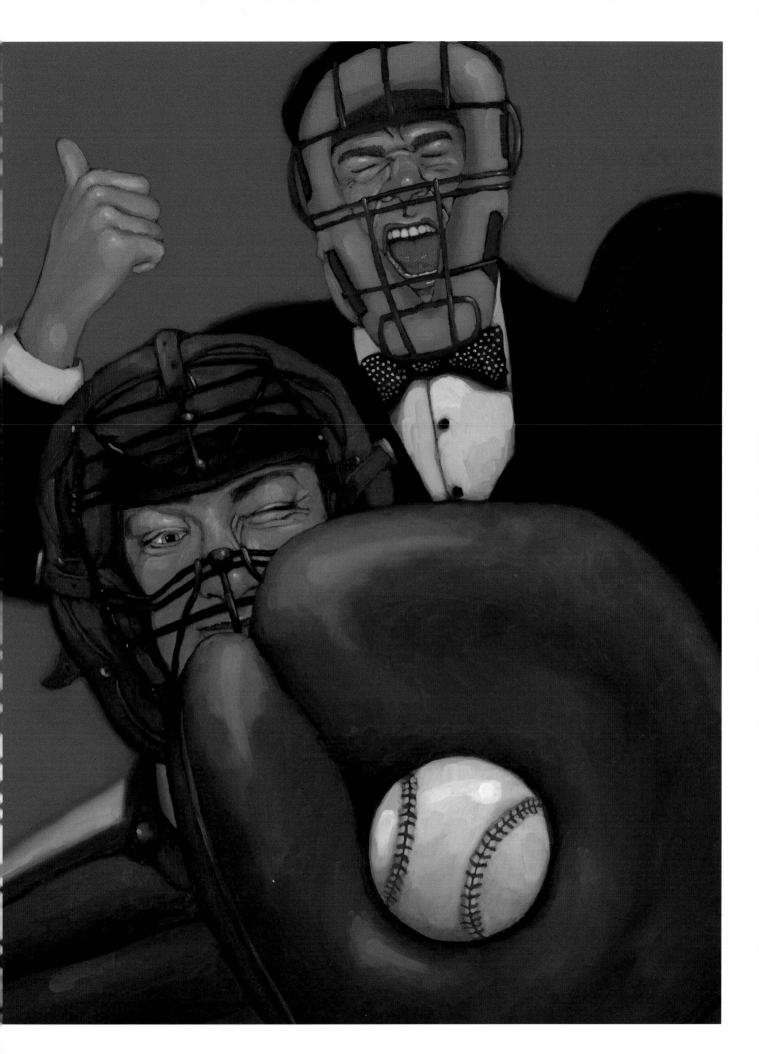

At the
OLD
BALL
GAME!"

"There will never be another Matty ... Christy Mathewson brought something to baseball no one else had ever given the game ... a certain touch of class, an indefinable lift in culture, brains, personality."

—Grantland Rice, sportswriter

During the September 23rd contest, in the bottom of the ninth inning, the Giants were up to bat with two men out, two men on base, and the score tied. Al Bridwell smashed a single past second base, and base runner Moose McCormick (who was on third) headed home to bring in the winning run while Fred Merkle (who was substituting for injured Fred Tenney) headed toward second. In an explosive celebration, thousands of fans swarmed the field and the players. The New York Giants believed they had won the game—and perhaps the lead in the National League pennant race!

EXTRA INNINGS ⚾ ⚾ ⚾

The story's not over yet! Convinced of the Giants' victory, nineteen-year-old Fred Merkle headed toward the clubhouse without having touched second base. Witnessing this, Cubs second baseman Johnny Evers instructed teammates to retrieve the ball. Two Cubs wrestled the game day souvenir away from a Giants fan, heaved it to Tinker, who then sailed it to Evers. Jumping up and down on second base, Evers declared an out. After two days of consideration, the winning run was called back. The game was declared a draw (1-1), with a rematch to follow if both teams were tied for the pennant race at the end of the season. Remembered as the "Merkle Boner," the game is still considered the biggest blunder in the history of Major League Baseball. (For many years, the verb "merkle" was commonly used to mean "to not arrive.") The disputed match was rescheduled on October 8, 1908, at the Polo Grounds. The Cubs won the rematch 4-2 and the National League pennant. Manager John McGraw went to his grave claiming the pennant had been robbed from his team and never blamed Fred Merkle for the incident. Giants owner John T. Brush had gold medals created for his team that read: THE REAL CHAMPIONS 1908.

The Polo Grounds flooded with fans after the September 23, 1908, contest (courtesy of National Baseball Hall of Fame Library, Cooperstown, N.Y.)

THE GIANTS tied for second place in the National League in 1908, along with the Pittsburgh Pirates. The much-beloved team had an impressive record from 1885 to 1957, winning five World Series Championships and a record fifteen National League pennants before being sold to San Francisco in 1958. The Giants baseball team has not yet captured the World Series Championship since leaving the Big Apple.

THE CUBS swept the 1907 and 1908 World Series, winning both titles in five games each. The success of these two years has not yet been repeated in Chicago, but love for the team continues to thrive there.

THE POLO GROUNDS were demolished in 1964 by the same wrecking ball that demolished The Brooklyn Dodgers' Ebbets Field. Today, four apartment buildings named The Polo Grounds Towers stand where the field was once located. A cement playground lies where deep hits to center field once landed.

CHRISTY MATHEWSON continued to pitch for the Giants until being traded to the Cincinnati Reds, where he played, then managed, from 1916 to 1918. He then returned to coach the Giants from 1919 to 1920. His columns about baseball appeared in New York newspapers, and with John N. Wheeler he produced several books on the art of twirling. He died on October 7, 1925, at the age of 45. His plaque at Baseball's Hall of Fame reads: MATTY WAS MASTER OF THEM ALL.

SOURCES The incidents here have been documented in such volumes as Christy Mathewson's *Pitching in a Pinch: Baseball from the Inside* (Lincoln: University of Nebraska Press, 1994); Noel Hynd's *Giants of the Polo Grounds: The Glorious Times of Baseball's New York Giants* (New York: Doubleday, 1987); Geoffrey C. Ward and Ken Burns's *Baseball: An Illustrated History* (New York: Knopf, 1996); David W. Anderson's *More than Merkle: A History of the Best and Most Exciting Baseball Season in Human History* (Lincoln: University of Nebraska Press, 2000); David Nemec's *Great Baseball Feats, Facts & Firsts* (New York: Signet Sports, 2003); G. H. Fleming's *The Unforgettable Season: The Most Exciting & Calamitous Pennant Race of All Time* (New York: Holt, Rinehart and Winston, 2000); Gil Bogen's *Tinker, Evers and Chance: A Triple Biography* (Jefferson, N.C.: McFarland & Company, Inc., 2003); Bill James's *The New Bill James Historical Baseball Abstract: The Classic—Completely Revised* (New York: Free Press, 2003); Burt Solomon's *The Baseball Timeline: In Association with Major League Baseball* (New York: Dorling Kindersley, 2001); and Lawrence S. Ritter's *Lost Ballparks: A Celebration of Baseball's Legendary Fields* (New York: Viking Studio Books, 1994).

QUOTES Page 10: Fleming, *The Unforgettable Season.* Page 12: Ward and Burns, *Baseball: An Illustrated History.* Page 15: "Player Stats," http://www.baseball-almanac.com. Page 20: Fleming, *The Unforgettable Season.* Page 23: Tinker quote from Mathewson, *Pitching in a Pinch;* Mathewson quote from Bogen, *Tinker, Evers and Chance.* Page 24: "Christy Mathewson Quotes," http://www.brainyquote.com/quotes/authors/c/christy_mathewson.html; *New York Press* quote from Fleming, *The Unforgettable Season.* Page 26: Fleming, *The Unforgettable Season.* Page 28: Mathewson, *Pitching in a Pinch.* Page 30: "Christy Mathewson Quotes," http://www.christymathewson.com/quote.html.

TAKE ME OUT
TO THE BALL GAME

Lyrics by Jack Norworth ⚾ Composed by Albert Von Tilzer

BEAU, N.Y., FAN

CASEY, N.Y., FAN

BUCKNELL, N.Y., FAN

MERKLE, N.Y., NAT'L*

*Where is Fred Merkle? Read the last page of the book to find out!